How God Fix Jonah

To My friend Herb Lotter —and
Enjoy my father's stories —and
may your heart lay down.

Ruth
Christmas 2005

Also by Lorenz Graham

How God Fix Jonah

by Lorenz Graham
Illustrated by Ashley Bryan

Foreword by W. E. B. Du Bois
New Foreword by Effie Lee Morris

Boyds Mills Press

Published by Caroline House
Boyds Mills Press, Inc.
A Highlights Company
815 Church Street
Honesdale, Pennsylvania 18431
Printed in China

U.S. Cataloging-in-Publication Data
  (Library of Congress Standards)

Graham, Lorenz B.
    How God fix Jonah / by Lorenz Graham ; illustrated by Ashley
Bryan. —1st ed.
  [160] p. : col. illus. ; cm.
Text originally published NY: Reynal & Hitchcock, 1946.
Summary: A collection of Bible stories told in the idiom of West Africa.
ISBN: 1-56397-698-6
1. Bible stories. 2. Folk literature, African. I. Bryan, Ashley,
ill. II. Title.
220.9/505 --21 2000   AC CIP
99-68099

First revised edition, 2000
The text of this book is set in 14-point Goudy.
The illustrations are blockprints.

Visit our Web site at www.boydsmillspress.com

10 9 8 7 6 5 4 3 2

To the memory of Lorenz Graham
—A. B.

Contents

Foreword

As I thought about how to approach writing this appreciation of Lorenz Graham and his work, I was reminded of his early contributions and how he gave so much of himself to his writing.

I knew him during the latter part of his life and understood his commitment when I learned he was the son of an African Methodist Episcopal minister. He had interrupted his studies at the University of California at Los Angeles to go to Africa to teach in an African Methodist Episcopal missionary school in Liberia in West Africa.

Lorenz Graham was always interested in writing and was encouraged by his older sister, Shirley, who was later married to Dr. W. E. B. Du Bois. By 1946 he had published *Tales of Momolu*, stories about the life of an African boy, and had also published *How God Fix Jonah*. Bible stories, like those in Lorenz Graham's collection, had been told by the students and teachers in the missionary schools. As storytelling is used as a method of teaching, the children tried to reproduce the sounds of the English language as they heard the missionaries speak it.

The language is poetic and rhythmical and includes African cultural contexts. The students and teachers had adapted the stories to include the human conditions as they knew them. Can you hear in your imagination the voice of an African boy retelling these stories with the laughter, the intonation, and the enunciation of his people?

With two books published in one year, it was then that Lorenz Graham decided that writing about the African people and African Americans would be an important part of his future life.

This was part of his background when he came to San Francisco in 1969 during the Civil Rights period. He was a member of the all-black Group of Five, who had been subsidized by publishers for the first major children's program about Negroes at San Francisco Public Library. I enjoyed his words and his wisdom.

He spoke about his Town book series of contemporary African American life, which was deemed controversial by the publishers because of his approach to racism in the stories. He spoke with controlled anger, but not bitterness, of his difficulties finding a publisher for his series. Lorenz was a delightful speaker with a quick wit and a quick smile, a thoroughly approachable person. He was a gentle person and a dignified gentleman of wisdom.

Lorenz Graham was a pioneer—an unsung hero who persevered despite rejections and disappointments. He made a major contribution to children's literature about black people in Africa and the United States.

How God Fix Jonah is an important historical representation of the language and culture of Africa and has a place with other interpretations of the Bible. How delighted I am that this important book, with its original preface by Dr. W. E. B. Du Bois and art by Ashley Bryan, is being reissued for the pleasure of current and future generations.

In his quiet, steadfast, hopeful way, Lorenz Graham is smiling.

Effie Lee Morris
Former Coordinator Children's Services
San Francisco Public Library

Foreword to the 1946 Edition

These little poems are bits of literature that now and then bring us insight into the working of the minds of men. The stories of the Christ child, of Jonah, Ruth, Job, Solomon, and other Biblical characters are told here in the words and thought patterns of a modern African boy who does not know Western civilization and does not use the conventional words and phrases that by long usage often obscure the meaning of these tales in the minds of Europeans and Americans.

This is the stuff of which literature is made; and in the lore of the world, the literature of Africa has its place, although this is often forgotten. Climate, the slave trade, and the Industrial Revolution have made the preservation of African literature dependent more on tradition and folklore than on written record. These modern bits of poetry rescued from passing oblivion remind us of what Africa has thought and done in the long past. It may also help us to realize that even today Africa is news. How could it be otherwise on the continent where civilization first started; which Greece and Rome respected and the Middle Ages held on terms of equality? Finally, Africa gave the toil that made America and underlay the modern era.

W. E. B. Du Bois
New York City

Introduction

These stories from the Bible are offered in the idiom of the West African native. Among people who are without the printed word, the spoken narrative is an important cultural unit. In Africa professional storytellers move from village to village with their tales. Passing strangers are invited to tell their stories. The villagers who go into the outside world and come back again must tell their experiences and repeat what they have heard. These stories are set down as an African lad might tell them to his friends.

He speaks in the vernacular of those who have been under the influence of European civilization. His English is the dialect understood by members of coastal tribes of Mandingos and Krus and Golahs. It has some basic similarities in pronunciation to the dialect of the plantation Negro in the American southland. There are two notable similarities and there are several distinctive differences.

In the primitive Sudanic tongues there is no equivalent for our *th* diphthong, and when the African says *this* and *that* he pronounces "dis" and "dat." Our *think* he pronounces "tink" and *thing* becomes "ting." Another striking similarity is his muting of the final *r* sound. In the southern states where *r* is muted after the vowel sound, there is a substitution of a soft open vocalization. *More* is pronounced in the South as "moah" to rhyme with Noah. In Africa it is "mo" with no apology for the absent *r*.

The variations are many. *The* is always pronounced with a hard *d* sound and with the long *e*. *Ing* as a suffix to the verb is not used a great deal, but when it does appear it receives a generous ring as though the sound were pleasant to the speaker. He almost smacks his lips after bringing it out.

He serves often for female and neuter as well as masculine. *Him* is both objective and possessive. *She* is used as possessive and objective as well as nominative, and *we* likewise serves in the three cases.

Some of the words used in their English dialect were left on the coast by early Spanish and Portuguese slave traders two hundred years ago.

Palaver is one of these. *Palabra* translates from Spanish as "word" but in the vernacular palaver has a wider meaning. It includes the thought of many words as in discussion or conducting of business. Sometimes it suggests trouble, as when the two mothers take their palaver to wise King Solomon. In the story of the lad David "war palaver catch the country" and the people are involved in the troublesome business of fighting. In the story of Joseph "woman palaver" lands the young man in jail. In the African community, the town meeting place is called the "palaver house." In its shelter court is held, announcements are made, stories are told. Palaver is a useful and oft repeated word among the people.

Another Spanish contribution is the verb for "to know," used also in the American argot. *Savvy* is used in Africa for "to know" and "to understand," more often to express understanding than knowledge.

Pican, used up and down the coast for baby or son or child, comes from the roots that result in "picaninny." *Pequeño* is Spanish for "small" and *niño* signifies "son." From the Spanish *pequeño niño*, the African adopted pican, and today he holds it tenderly to his bosom. "Picaninny" is sometimes heard where natives are currently in close communication with Americans or Europeans. Perhaps they look upon the longer as proper talk.

A number of words are brought to his English direct from the tribal tongue. For the reader's sake such expressions have not been used in these stories except for an occasional word highly expressive of a characteristic that seems to translate into sound.

Wa-wa connotes mischief or naughtiness. The "wa-wa woman" is dangerous to domestic bliss. The "wa-wa town" is running fast and loud. The "wa-wa boy" does not follow in the good father's footsteps.

The speech is basically rhythmic and poetic. It flows with a beat. Apparently without effort on the part of the speaker the arrangements fall of themselves into place. The article is in or it is out as fits the rhythm. There seems to be no rule or any other justification for arbitrary use or omission.

Verbs are usually used in the present tense. Past is indicated when necessary by the past of the verb "to do" and futurity is shown by the use of "will." Sometimes it does appear that the auxiliary "do" or "done" is inserted only for reason of the rhythm.

It is this sense of rhythm that makes the African narrator give a story from the Bible as a poem, or shall we say a spoken song. He sings his story.

He enjoys the euphony of the words. Words are chosen from a small vocabulary with few coloring adjectives or adverbs, but the song is sung and it is sweet. The pictures are sharp. The story is clear and the hearer can easily repeat it. Those who read the stories may find that memorizing a page is little more than the work of reading it aloud, and if a line should not be quoted as set down in the book the new arrangement may be better. Who can say?

Little attempt has been made to break the spelling into phonetic representation of the African's pronunciation. *The* may be read conventionally or as "de." The sound of *r* after the vowel may be used or omitted. The idiom, the word pictures, the beauty of the simple thought will be the same. As in all poetry the greatest pleasure will be in reading the stories aloud.

Then read aloud and picture standing before you an African lad who has heard the old stories of gods and devils and loud-spoken kings and fearless slaves. Hear him say,

Long time past
Before them big tree live
Before them big tree's papa live
That time God live.

—Lorenz Graham

How God Fix Jonah

How God Fix Jonah

Jonah was a prophet.
God put Him hand on Jonah
But Jonah head be hard.
Jonah head be hard too much.

Lord God Almighty can fix the thing.
Can fix hard head
Can fix weak back
Can fix crooked leg.
God can fix anything.

Hear how He fix Jonah.

God say, "Jonah, O Jonah!"
Jonah say, "Yea Lord!"
God say, "Jonah
Go down to Nineveh and preach My Word."

Nineveh be one wa-wa place
And Jonah fear that town too much.
And he fear God, but small.
He make like he go, but he hide.

Jonah go to the waterside
He look them boats what sail.
He say to cap'n for one boat, "What side you go?"
The man say, "Nineveh."
Jonah say, "No."

Nother cap'n come and Jonah say, "What side you go, man?"
The man say, "Tarsus."
Jonah climb aboard
And when the boat shove off he lay down low
And on the waterside no man can see him.

Lord God Almighty say, "Ho!"
When God say "Ho" it make a mighty wind
And waves run on the boat
And rock it so the crew mens fear.

The crew mens do all that they can.
They throw the cargo overboard
They take in sail
They put out oars
They hold, they pull,
But all the time more water come inside.
They fear.

The crew mens say the waters want somebody on the boat.
They make a trial with sassa wood to see what man bring
       trouble.
They watch the stick go round about
And pass up all but Jonah.

And Jonah say,
      "For true.
      The palaver be on my own head for true.
      I run to hide from Lord God Almighty
      Who rule all the wind and run all the water.
      But if I make my bed in hell
      I know He find me."

Lord God Almighty say "Ho" again.
The wind holler louder
The water rise higher
And all men see His power.

Then the cap'n and the crew mens take a hold on Jonah.
They lift him up and throw him in the sea.
It make the boat ride easy.
The wind go soft and still
The sea make like a river.

The crew mens look about and say, "Lord God Almighty!"

God say, "Jonah, O Jonah!"
Jonah say, "Yea, Lord!"
God say, "Jonah,
Go down to Nineveh and preach My Word."

Jonah don't know where at he live.
But God done make a special fish
When the crew mens throw Jonah overboard
That fish take Jonah up.

Three days the fish ride Jonah.
The fish carry man in him belly
Three days, and Jonah ain't savvy.
The fish carry Jonah to the Nineveh beach.

Lord God Almighty talk to the fish.
The fish open up and puke Jonah out.
Jonah wash in the sea and dry in the sun
And he go to Nineveh to preach the Word.

Good in She Heart

Now I'm going tell you bout Ruth.

First time Ruth's people ain't know bout God
Ruth self ain't know bout the true God
But Ruth be good in she heart.
She do right for all people
She ain't hurt nobody
She heart lay down.

But lemme tell you bout it.

One time down in Judah land
The rain, it come too soon,
Soon before the farm was made.
And when the rain stop
It stop too soon
And the small farm spoil.
And when the people look for chop
They can't find nothing
And there be some sit down and cry
And there be some go for nother country
Cause they hongry.

There be one man that time
What go for Moab country
He take him wife
And he take him two sons.
All four, they walk plenty
Cause the Moab country be far.
They ain't got plenty chop
And the old man no be strong.
Sick palaver put him hand
On the old man heart
And the old man holler
But he die.

But the old lady she got strong heart
She live good in the Moab country.
And bye-m-bye the sons
They see fine Moab womans and like em
And they take Moab womans for wife.
The wife for one name Orpah
And the wife for nother one name Ruth
And the old lady name be Naomi.

Bye-m-bye sick palaver catch all two the men
And sick palaver squeeze they heart
And they holler and they fight.
But the chill be strong
And the fever be strong

And the sick palaver be strong past all
And they die.

Then the old lady cry too much.
All she friends in the Moab country
Come look on the Judah woman
But she heart want go for Judah land.

So Naomi call the two womens
Who was wifes for them two boys
And she make the palaver for them.
Hear how Naomi talk for the young womans.
      "Orpah,
      You was good for me, hyeah.
      Ruth,
      You was good for me, hyeah.
      You was good for me
      And you was good for my picans.
      I love you plenty.

      "But now my man he dead
      Now you mens they dead
      All dead.
      I must go back for my Judah country
      I think so you must go back to you pa's house.
      God bless you, hyeah.

You good too much.
God bless you, hyeah."

Orpah and Ruth they cry
They say
　　"No,
　　Our hearts no going lay down if we left you.
　　We must go with you
　　We must go with you back for Judah land."

Naomi talk some more again.
　　"How now?
　　You think so I got more pican for my belly?
　　You think so you can wait for them for husband?
　　No no
　　Don't do so.
　　Go for you home
　　Find you new mens.
　　You be young so find new mens.
　　Go now."

Orpah, she cry small
She kiss the old lady
She head hang down but she go.
But Ruth ain't go
She hold on.

"No, no, no, I can't left you."
And Naomi say
    "You ain't see your sister done go?"

But Ruth fall down and cry
She hold Naomi's foot.
Long time she cry and when she talk
She talk like this.
    "Ay-bah, Mommy!
    Don't beg me to left you
    Don't beg me to go back.
    Cause the place where you go
    I want go.
    The place where you stay
    I want stay.
    You people
    I want know em for my people.
    You God
    I want have Him for my God.
    The place where you die
    I going die
    And the same place they going bury me.
    I swear fore God, Mommy,
    I ain't never going left you."

So that's how come
Ruth come for Judah land.

He No Be Keeper
for Him Brother

Abel be a cattle man
And in him heart he clean and good.
And all he do God bless
And he love God.

He make a fire at him holy place
And make him sacrifice and pray.
He bring the finest cow he got
To kill and burn for God.

Cain be Abel's brother.
He dig and plant and make a farm
And Earth be good for him
And give him plenty crop.

Cain go to make him sacrifice
But in him heart he small and mean.
He no want give God anything.
He say
        "I no going burn good chop
        I no be fool."

All two the fires burn.
All two the mens bow down.
God hear when Abel pray
And send the breeze
To make the fire bright
To shine on Abel's house
And make him heart lay down.

On other side Cain bring
One bag old rice he no can trade
One tin palm oil what done spoil
One coconut what no got water
And one casaba.

Cain burn him gift
But God hold back the breeze.
The smoke scwonge all about
And when Cain try to pray
He choke.

Cain rise and walk about
And when he see him brother pray in peace
And how God bless him house
And make the fire burn so bright
Him evil heart turn over.

He lift a rock and break him brother head
And with a knife he cut him brother neck.
And then he fear.
He look—
Nobody see the thing.
He bury Abel in the field
And hide inside him house.

Cain fear people and he hide from people
But it be God what know.
When people come and say
        "Where be you brother?"
Cain fool them and he say
        "He walk about for nother side."
Else he say "He go into far country."

And people can believe
But you no fool God.
God put Him hand on Cain
He say
        "Wait—
        This be God palaver
        Where be you brother?"

Cain look about to run
He no can move him foot
He make like it no be for him.
He say

"You think so
I be keeper for my brother?
It be my part to savvy where my brother go
And all he do
You think so?"

God say
"For true you savvy.
For true I savvy too
The earth done open up she mouth
To drink you brother blood
And that same mouth cry out
To tell me what you do."

God put Him mark on Cain
So all men know he kill him brother.
And when he dig and plant a farm
The earth hold back the crop
And Cain be hongry.

David He No Fear

David mind the sheep for him pa.
Every day he drive the sheep
He find good grass
He find sweet water
He mind the sheep good.

David don't humbug nobody
And most times nobody don't humbug David.
When he mind the sheep him heart lay down
And he make songs.
He make songs and he sing him songs.
He make harp with plenty strings
He play him harp
He sing.

Bye-m-bye the war palaver catch Judah country
And all the mens must go.
The young men
The strong men
Take up spear and cutlass
And they go.
David's brothers go
But David self no be a man

So he stay by and mind the sheep,
David and him pa.
Bye-m-bye the word come back
The word say war go bad for Judah.
The word say other people be strong too much
And giant be for their side
No Judah man can fight him.
And David hear the word.

David go fore him pa face.
He say
  "Pa,
   Make it I go find my brothers.
   Make it I carry them chop
   They can be hongry this time."
The old man say "I agree."
When David come to the place
He walk about to find him brothers
And while he look he hear somebody say
   "Oh! One man make war for we!"

Then David see the giant.
He be high past ten men
He be strong same way
He got iron helmet on him head
And more iron on him front.
He walk about and laugh

He say
>"Ho-ho-ho!
>Them funny Judah mens!
>They no can fight.
>Come out now so I kill you
>And if you no can fight
>Go home and find you mommies.
>Ho-ho-ho!"

And Judah mens do fear for true.
The Judah mens they fear to fight the giant
But David, he no fear.
David take him sling
He pick up round hard rocks
He walk out fore the giant and say
>"We God going fight for we!"

The giant say
>"Ho! Small boy done come to say how-do."

David say
>"I come for fight!"

Giant say
>"Do you mommy know you out?"

David say
>"Now I kill you!"

Giant say
>"Go from my face less I eat you!"

David stand.
He put rock in him sling
He turn it all about and round and round.
The giant coming close
The sling leggo.
Hmmmmm . . . . Bop!

The giant holler out
He hold him head
He turn.
He try to walk
He fall.
He roll
He twist about
He die.

David walk up close
While all the Judah people shout
And all the other people run.
David take the giant cutlass self
And cut the giant head from off him neck.
Then David's brothers come and say
    "You fool!
    The war palaver be for men.
    Go home!
    Go home and mind the sheep."
And David say "Now I go."

Don't Nobody Sing

When David be the king
He see every kind of humbug
Set down in him house.

He make war and plenty good mens die.
He set up chiefs and council men
And they play rogue.
He got one son who turn away
And make him plenty trouble.
The son make war against the pa
And every time him pa want peace
The boy be hard.

But David love him son
And when he go for war he say
        "All my mens
        Hear my word!
        My son Absalom make war for me
        But I say nev mind
        He be my son
        I love him.
        All my mens
        Hear my word!

When you go fight
No man must hurt my son.
If any do
Him will I kill
And throw him bones to dogs.
Hear my word."

All the soldiers hear
And go to mind.
But when the war be hot
And plenty people fall
And every man must kill or die
Young Absalom be in a tree
And soldiers come behind with spears
And kill him.
Him people run away
And war be finish.

One man run to tell the king
The war be finish
And him people win.
King David say
    "My son,
      He live?"
The man he fear and say
He no can tell
Cause plenty people die.

Another man come with the word.
King David say again
  "My son,
  He live?"
The soldier say
  "Every son what raise him hand
  To fight him pa
  Must die.
  So it be with Absalom!"

King David turn about.
Him head hang down
He cry.
And when he turn again
The people see he be
A tired, weak old man.

He say
  "Don't nobody sing
  Don't nobody beat a drum
  Don't nobody cry."
The old man lay him fine clothes by.
He put on country cloth
And softly climb the steps
To one dark room inside him house.

The people hear him say
    "O Absalom,
    My son, my son,
    Make it God kill me
    So you can live."

Nobody don't sing
Nobody don't beat a drum
Nobody don't cry.

God Wash the World and Start Again

You talking bout the time!
You think you see some rain!
You vex to see the water falling so
On the house!

God make the time for Him Own Self.

He make the rain
He make the dry and wet.
He make the sunny day
And dark of night for rest.
This time He make it good for we
And rainy day can come and go
And all be dry again
And people live.
But was a time
When all the world be young,
A so-so long time past,
That God let all the rain fall down
And cover up the land
And every house and tree

And every hill and mountain.
The rain done fall that time for true.

First time God make the world
And all the mens
And all the thing that move about.
First time Him heart lay down
But bye-m-bye He look and see
The people no be fit to hear Him Word
And things what walk be bad too much
And God want try again.

God see mens what grow like trees
And elephants like mountains walk about
And leopards big like elephant
And monkey mens what eat the people
And snakes what carry fire in their mouth
To cook the mens they eat.

And God no like to see the world be so.

In all the world He see one man
What mind Him Word.
God go down and speak
He say
      "Noah, O Noah!
      Hear My Word.
      I want you cut down plenty trees

And make a ship.
I want it be the biggest ship
Man ever see.
I want it be from here to there
And plenty tight
And when you finish so
I come again."

Now Noah call him people,
All him sons and all the mens they got.
They set to cut down trees
And lay to build a ship
And people come and laugh.
They say
    "How now?
    This old man Noah build him ship
    Far from the sea.
    How now?
    Who going carry ship to water for him
    When he finish?
    He be fool!"

The people come and laugh
But Noah and him people build
And make it tight with pitch.
God come walk about inside the ship
And Noah hear God's Word and mind.
God say like this

"Noah, O Noah,
You make it here rooms
And here you make a cargo space
Just so."
Nother time God say
"Noah, O Noah,
That side you got bad board,
Make it your son take that one out."

And how God say, that way Old Noah do.
One day the ship be finish
All the people come to see.
The ship be big past anything before
And no water there.

God walk about with Noah on the ship.
He say
"Noah, O Noah,
You hear My Word
You make My heart lay down.
Now see what you must do.
Go take up in all the land
The things what walk
The things what crawl
The things what fly
Go catch them two by two."

So Noah call him people,

All him sons and all the mens they got,
They set to bring the living things
That walk and crawl and fly
They bring the man and woman kind
They bring them two by two.
They bring in corn and rice for chop.
They bring in elephant
They bring in cow and horse
And fowl and snake and goat
And dog and leopard,
Deer and monkey
And everything that move in bush
And in the air
They bring.
And God look on and call for something else
And something else they bring.
And God look on and know
The thing be good.

He say
        "Noah, O Noah,
        You done mind me good!
        Now go aboard and take you people,
        Seal the door and seal the hatch
        And wait!"

That time God open up the sky
And let the water fall
And all the world see water.

It no fall in rain that time
It pour down till all the world be full.
And rivers run in every road
And every field be like a lake
And every lake be like a sea
And all the low land fill.
And hills stand up like islands
And then the islands self done cover
And only mountains stand.
And soon the mountains cover up
And all the land and all the sea be all the same.

Where be the people what done laugh?
Where be the giants what walk like trees?
Where be the leopards big like elephants?
And all the elephants standing up like mountains?
Where they be?
God look down on all the water
And then he hold the rain.
God look down and all he find
Be Noah's one ship on the sea.
In that one ship live everything that live
Above the water.

God say
        "Now!
        My old world done finish.

I make new start
And everything I do
I look him good."
God open new holes down in the sea
To drain the land.
He make the sun shine bright
And send dry winds
To sweep the world.

 He put the ship down softly
And see Noah with His people
And all the things that walk
And things what crawl
And things what fly
Go out again.

He smile
And in the sky He set Him bow
And turn to make a better world.

Samson He Weak for Woman Palaver

Samson!
Samson be a man—oh
Samson!

Samson be strong past every other man.
He be strong in him foot
He be strong in him leg
He be strong in him hip
He be strong in him back
He be strong in him arm
But—oh!
Samson he be weak,
He be weak for the woman palaver.

Samson!
Samson see a woman
Down in Phillistown
And he go good for she.
Samson take the woman for him wife
But she fool him
Oh she fool him good
And put the shame palaver on him face.
Then she laugh.

Samson catch him plenty fox.
Three hundred fox he catch.
He tie some fire on they tail
And loose them in the farm.
He loose the fox with fire on behind
In every field with rice in Phillistown
And then he left.

Him brothers come to Samson in him house
And say that they must tie him up
Or Phillistown going make a war
And burn they farms and break they house
To make them just the same.
The brothers tie up Samson tight
But when the people come to take him way
He rise up and he break the rope
And take a jawbone from a hoss
And kill a thousand men.

Samson!
Samson be a man—oh
But Samson he be weak,
He be weak for the woman palaver.

Samson go to Gaza
And love a woman there
But she fool him—
Oh she fool him, too.

And when he sleeping in she house
She call the Gaza men
And they lock the big gate in the Gaza wall.

Samson rise.
Samson rise and make to go
And he find the gate be tight
So he pull the gate-post out
With the gate all locked together.
And he put them on him head
And he carry them away
And he set them up again on a hill
Far away.

Samson!
Samson be a man—oh
He be strong past every other man
But Samson he be weak,
He be weak for the woman palaver.

Samson see Delilah
And she be fat and fine
But she wa-wa.
She fool him,
Oh she fool him
And plenty.

Delilah make she face and she say
    "You be strong
    You be big and pretty
    And I love you.
    But tell me how you be so strong
    And why no man can hurt you,
    Tell me fore I love you good some more."

Samson say
    "If they tie me with seven
    new green vines I no
    can lift my hand."

While Samson sleep
Delilah bring the mens and they tie him
Then Delilah clap she hands and she say
    "Wake up, Samson,
    The men done come from Phillistown."

Samson jump up quick and kill the mens what tie him
And he laugh.
Delilah poke out she mouth
She say
    "You done fool me, that I see
    You no love me
    When all the time I love you good.
    I no going love you gain.

Tell me now for true-true
How come you be so strong
Tell me now so I love you more."

He left Delilah and he walk about
But he think.
He think that she be fat and fine
And he weak and he come.
But Delilah no want play
And she poke she mouth and push him.
She say
      "I no going love you more till you tell me."

Samson!
Samson be a man—oh
But Samson he be weak,
He be weak for the woman palaver.

Samson say
      "I tell you now for true
      The thing live for the hair on my head.
      I no cut him.
      If I cut my hair away
      All the strong will left me too
      And I be weak.
      Now you savvy
      Now you love me good."

Delilah take him in she house
And love him.
She hold him head and she sing a song
She rub him softly softly and he sleep.
She hold him head and cut him hair
She cut it clean so all him strong can left him.

Delilah calls the mens
And they tie him.
Then she clap she hands and say
      "Wake up, Samson,
        The mens done come from Phillistown."

So it be when he want rise
He be weak.
He be small boy for the mens
And they take him.
They tie him on a stick
And they carry him for jail
And they beat him and they mark him
And they cut him in him eyes.

And they say
      "Samson!
      Samson be a man—oh
      But Samson he be weak,
      He be weak for the woman palaver."

Bye-m-bye the king
Make big day for mansion house.
He send all about to bring them other kings
And the big mens from all the country.
And when they eat plenty meat and drink plenty wine
The king say
    "Samson!
    Bring Samson in to stand before my face
    So we make play.
    That Samson what be strong past other mens
    That Samson what go about and kill my people
    That Samson what be weak for the woman palaver
    Bring him in."

They bring him
And the king call slaves to beat him
And the king call womens to fool him.
He be old man now and he shaky.
Him hair done grow again
And it be white.
He stand up tween two post
And he say
    "Now I must rest."

See him resting now
The man what done be strong

The man what done be weak.
He turn him dead eyes up to God and pray
And God send back him power
And strong come in him back
And in him arm and leg.

See him holding on them post.
He hold them tight
He pull them hard
He break them loose.
The top side go to fall
The outside fall
The king and all him people mash
And all the people die.

Samson!
Oh, Samson!
He be strong past all the other mens.
But Samson he be weak,
He be weak for the woman palaver.

Hongry Catch the Foolish Boy

They be one man what have two sons.
The young son go fore him pa face and he say,
"Pa, make it you give me that part what belong me."
The old man do so.

The young man take up them thing what belong him
And he go.
He go in country where people ain't know him.
He go in country where people ain't know him pa.
The people see him come
The people say
    "Oh!
      He got plenty fine cloth
      He got plenty gold bangles
      He got plenty money
      He be big man for true-true."

The boy have plenty friends
He have plenty fun
Bye-m-bye money finish.

He look about.
Them people live for friends, no live again.
Then hongry time come on the country

He no got house
He no got chop.
He go fore Mandingo man for beg small chop.
Mandingo man send him in field to mind hogs.

He be poor boy now.
He want fight hogs to eat hog chop.

He sit down. He think.
He think good for him head.
Bye-m-bye he hear somebody say
"How many people work for you pa?"
He say "Plenty."

He think again
And he hear somebody say
"The people what work for you pa,
Do hongry catch them people?"
He say "No."

He look at him self.
He no got robe for cover him skin.
He look at them hog, the hog no got robe same way.
He rise up like a man, he say
"I go. I go for my pa.
I will say

'Pa, I bring shame-palaver on you head
And in you house.
I no fit for be you son.
Make it I be like them what work for you.
Hongry done catch me.' "

So he turn back to the country where him pa live.

When the old man look up and see the boy come
Him heart turn over.
He run like small boy
He hold him son tight
He kiss him.

The boy cry. He say
        "Pa, I bring shame-palaver on you head
        And in you house.
        I no fit for be you son again.
        I come cause hongry catch me."

But the old man call the people and he say
        "Bring the best robe and put it on him
        Bring gold ring for him finger
        Bring shoes for him foots.
        Kill cow. Kill chicken. Kill goat.
        We going eat meat and drink palm wine
        We going make music, we going dance.

My pican was dead and now he live.
My pican was lost and now he found."

Now the first-born son,
He work hard in the rice farm that day.
The sun be plenty hot
The sweat run down.
While he work he hear the drums,
He come see what the palaver be.
The people say
      "You brother done come.
      The old man happy too much.
      He done kill that fat cow.
      He say all people must come for make play."

The boy vex.
He no want make play.
He tell him pa
      "How you do me so?
      All of this time I sit down by your hand,
      I work, I work, I work, I never left you.
      All of this time you never kill
      One small goat for me.
      How you do me so?
      That one bring shame on your head
      But when he come you be happy,
      You make feast for him."

The old man come close.

He put him hand on him boy's head.
He cry small and he say
    "For true,
    You be my pican what make my heart lay down.
    You be my first-born son.
    All the thing belong me, belong you same way.
    But see your brother,
    He was dead and now he live.
    He ain't got nothin
    And he hongry."

The first-born say
    "Old man,
    I come."

Pican in River Grass

The Hebrew people live in Egypt.
The Egypt people make them slaves
But God done bless the Hebrews
The slaves grow strong and plenty.

King Pharaoh make hard law for slaves
But they still be strong.
The masters make the Hebrews work too much
But picans keep on borning.

King Pharaoh say
    "This vex me plenty.
    Bye-m-bye the slaves going to take the country
    From the masters.
    Now I make new law
    And all must hear my word:
    The boy picans in every Hebrew house must die.
    The Hebrew mommies self must kill them
    Else soldiers go and break the house
    And kill all people in it.
    This be my law!"

You think so law can make a mommy kill she child?

God done bless one woman
And when she look on she small pican face
She heart be full.
She say
  "Not me,
  Not nobody going kill my child."

She keep the pican close inside she house
And don't say nothing.
Bye-m-bye the word say soldiers coming.
They coming to the town to see all people.
The mommy's heart turn over but she say
  "Not no soldier going kill my child."

The mommy take one basket
And she make him like a boat,
Bottom and side she make him tight with pitch
And in the basket country cloth
And over top the basket fine soft cloth.
She make him so to hide the pican
In the river grass.
So she hide him
And she set young gal to watch and she say
  "Not nobody going kill my child."

God see the small boat
And God know the cap'n what ride inside
And God send Pharaoh's daughter to that place.

She go to wash she skin
She go there with she women
And when she lay off all she clothes
She splash about and play.

She stop cause she hear something
When she look she find the basket
And she heart make big inside
When she see the pican laying there and crying.

Then the small gal what be for guard, she hide.
She hide but she see and she got plenty sense.
She walk out like she don't know nothing.
She see the princess holding pican
So she say
       "Oh!
       Mommy got fine pican
       But I no see nurse.
       Hebrew mommy make good nurse.
       You want me call a nurse?"
The gal got sense you know.
The gal call the mommy for the child
To be nurse.
The mommy say
       "Bless God!
       Ain't nobody going kill my child!"

God Make a Road
Down in the Sea

The Egypt people hold the Hebrews tight
And make them slaves
And make them work the farm
And work the road
And work some kind of hard.

The Hebrews cry
And sometimes they fall down and die
And all the time they moan and pray
And say "How long, O God, how long?"

God see the thing.
He hear Him people pray
And so He raise up Moses and He say
     "Moses,
     You the one
     To go fore Old King Pharaoh.
     You the one to carry him My Word.
     Tell King Pharaoh that I say
     'Let My people go!'
     Tell him,
     'Let My people go!' "

King Pharaoh no want hear that Word
But God put Him hand there
And take the Hebrews out.
He take them all,
The mens, the womens,
The old ones and the young.
He take them out from Egypt land
He start them back to Canaan
And Moses be they leader.

Now Moses never see that side before
And he don't know the way.
God say
       "Moses,
       Nev mind.
       I set My mark up in the sky
       You walk the way I show.
       By day My mark be in a cloud
       By night it be in fire."

And so they follow day by day
Across the sea of sand
And on the mountains
And in bush and swamp.
And they be plenty.

King Pharaoh come along behind
With all him army to make war
To take the Hebrews back for slaves again.
They come up close.
The Hebrews move out fast at night.
The soldiers come again.
The Hebrews move by day and night.
The soldiers come some more.
The Hebrews fear and run and then they reach a sea,
They reach a sea they no can cross.
They stop and cry.
    "How now?" they say.
    "How now?
    Moses done bring we here to die.
    We no can swim
    We no can find canoe
    We no can ride a steamer.
    How now?"

They cry and Moses self he fear
But Moses pray.

Now God can fix up anything.
God say
    "Moses, wait!

I show who rule the land and water
I show the people who can save them
I show all people who the true God be.
Wait!"
And Moses wait.

God say
    "Make the people meet Me on the beach!"
Moses do so.
God say
    "Moses,
    Hold out your stick,
    Hold it out over the water."
Moses do so.

Softly, softly east wind rise to blow.
It blow soft but with a force from God
And while the people look
They see the waters move.
Some water move one side and some the other
Some turn about and move and some move straight
Some move slow and some move quick
Some move in and some move out
Some come some go
But all do move.
While the people look

The waters open up and make a road down in the sea
While on two sides it rise and stand like mountains.
God say
> "Go!
> And while you go
> I will go with you!"

The people fear to go
But Moses lead
And one man go behind
Then two, then three, then plenty more,
And all the people follow through
And no man wet him foot.

When Pharaoh come he see the road
He see the Hebrews marching on.
He never see such thing before
He don't know God.
He say
> "I too will go
> And on the other side
> I take the Hebrew people.
> March!"
The army march.

They come on down the road
They no get wet till all the army march
With water high on one side and the other.

Then God reach down
And lay small trouble in the way
And men fall down and horses turn about.
The army stop.
The drummers beat they drums
The leaders call
The head men shout
The horn men blow they horns.
The king cry out.

Moses look down the road on the other side.
God speak softly to him.
Moses bow him head
He lift him stick
The waters go to move again
And water mountains fall and roll
And men cry out
While waves run high
And all the waters move about
Like they be vex.

And bye-m-bye a wave bring up King Pharaoh dead
And lay him down
At Moses foot.

They Be Slaves Too Long

When God bring Him people out from Egypt
He make road where no road live before
He give chop what no man taste before
He make sweet water come out from dry rock
He make the people walk a way where no man savvy.

God give the Word to Moses and Moses mind.
Moses take the people where God say
They no stop for make a house.
They walk, they walk, they walk,
They no scratch to make a farm,
They take the chop God give and all the time they move.
They be tired and they vex.

Some say
      "Who be this man Moses?
      What he think he be?
      We no be in Egypt land
      And he no be we master."

Some say
      "What side Moses take we now?
      Why we no can stay here?
      Every day we walk too much
      Let we make a town."

Some more say
> "Who give Moses power over we?
> Who say we must mind him?
> King Pharaoh make the Egypt law
> We no got king."

God hear everything they say.
He love Him people and He want show em
He call Moses and He say
> "Moses, hear My Word.
> Them people no savvy nothing
> They be slaves too long
> So hear Me good:
> Call you brother Aaron
> Let Aaron lead the people
> While you come set down by My hand
> And I make law."

Moses go one side high on the mountain
There he set down to hear God's Law.
God say
> "Tell the people
> I be they God
> What bring them out from Egypt.
> They no can have another god before Me
> They no can bow down or serve another God
> But Me One."
So God say.

Ten Laws He make
And then He make them plenty more.
He say how they must live in peace
How they must love they brother.
He say how they must work six days
And rest on Sundays and no work.
He say how they must marry
And how they make they court palaver.
And all the thing God say
Moses mark down on some rock.
He no got paper.

Moses setting on the mountain
To hear God's Law
He marking on the rock
All God say.
God ain't looking at the people
He ain't talking now to Aaron.

The people go fore Aaron
And they say
        "You see it ain't it.
        Moses done left we
        God done left we self.
        Make it you give we new god
        So we can pray.
        So we can call on new god
        To fight for we."

Aaron self ain't savvy
But he say "Wait!"

The people come again and say
        "Give we some kind of god."
Aaron look about, he no see Moses.
He look at the mountain, he ain't see God.
But he say "Wait!"

Bye-m-bye people come again
They say
        "Give we new god
        Else we be finish."

Aaron say
        "Bring gold
        From all you finger rings
        And all you ear rings
        And all you bangles.
        Bring gold
        I going make a god for you."
Aaron make fire and burn the gold
And he pour it and he beat it and he cut it.
So he make a cow and say
        "This be you god!"

When Moses come
He bring the rocks with all God's Law.
He hear the people where they sing

And beat they drums and dance.
He see the people bow to pray
Before the cow in holy place
And he be vex.

He throw down all them rock he carry for the Law.
He pull the gold cow down and break it up.
He cry out loud
      "Who be for the true God?"
When they see him plenty people come
To stand up by him side
And they take sword and spear
And go about to kill them people
Who want turn from God.
Ten thousand people die.

Then Moses go fore God and say
      "Oh them people make bad sin
      I want beg You now forgive them.
      But if You no can do so
      If You must break You people
      Break just me now
      And lemme die."

God say
      "Moses,
      I done call you for lead My people—
      Lead them then."

She Got Hard Head You Know

God look all about the world.
He see one town this side
Nother town He see that side
He see plenty field and plenty bush.

God hear some people pray
And then Him heart lay down.
He bless them.
He hear a woman cry for pain
He touch her and she sleep.

God passing by in peace
Until He come to Sodom Town
And Sodom stink.

God say
    "How it be?
    I no make My people so.
    How it be
    These people do so bad?"

God send Him angels there
He want them look to find
If any people in the town
Do mind God's Word.

They walk about in Sodom Town
And everywhere they walk the bad mens come behind
To make them trouble.
They find one man whose name be Lot
Who have good heart
And him they tell
    "Mind!
    God going fix the thing.
    God going take care of Sodom
    God going break the town
    And all the people in it.
    Rise up then and go your way
    Rise up and take your people
    Rise up and run for bush
    And don't look back."

And Lot say
    "Do this be God's Word!"
The angels say
    "For true!"

Lot call him people round him
But they say
    "Humbug!
    We no fear.
    We like this town
    We make plenty play
    We got plenty wine
    And what we no got for we self we take."

So Lot call him one wife
And he call him two young gals.
He say
> "We go with God
> And when we go
> We no look back,
> So the Word say."

But Lot's one wife she got hard head.
She no agree to left the place.
She no agree to say good-by to all she friends.
She come on slow.

She say
> "All of this time Lot stay in Sodom,
> All of this time I see some fun!"

She come on
But she come slow.

Lot walk on down the road
And Lot cry out
> "We go with God
> And when we go
> We no look back,
> So the Word say."

God see everything.
When Lot move out God open up
And fire fall from heaven on the town
And all the people in the house run out
And fire catch them in the street.
And people in the street run in the house
And fire burn up all the thatch
And more fire fall inside
And all the houses burn
And all the people die
And all the cattle.

Lot walk on the road.
He see the light.
He hear the fire burning
And he cry out
  "We go with God
  And when we go
  We no look back,
  So the Word say."

He no look back.
The young gals no look back.
Him wife, she got hard head you know,
She got to turn about and look.
While she look she fear
And all she blood run dry.

She hands be dry
She look and they be white.
She look she feet
And they be dry and white.
She dry up in she bones
She no can turn again.
She dry up in she mouth
She no can call.
And while she stand and look at Sodom burn
The woman self be no more meat but salt,
Dry, hard, white, so-so salt.

But Lot,
Lot and him two young gals,
They walk on down the road
And Lot cry out
      "We go with God
      And when we go
      We no look back,
      So the Word say."

Death Take Him Hand
Off Pican Heart

Elisha be God's prophet
What move about through all the country.
He carry God's Word
And people hear the Word and they mind.
The king self hear the Word
And him heart lay down.
God bless the nation
Peace live in the land.

One woman what be Shumanite
Live in the country.
She heart be fine and what she do be good
She trade and plenty people come
So she grow rich.
She hear the God palaver
When the prophet come, and she believe.

Bye-m-bye the woman Shumanite
Go to the man what she belong.
She say
      "I see the God man
      Every day, every day.

He walking all about to bring the Word
And when he come this side
He no got place for rest.
Make it then we put small house
On backside to we house
So God man can go in."
The man agree and it be so.

Elisha come again.
He go inside him house and take him rest
When he come out he say
"God bless you, hyeah,
You got good heart for me.
Now anything you say
If I can do, I do.
If any word
You want me speak on any side
I speak that word.
If anything you want the king for do
He be my friend
He do the thing I say.
Speak now."

The woman bow she head
She say
"You be God man
The Word you bring be sweet.

Now I love God
And God be good for me.
You country too be good for me
And all the people do me good.
God done bless my land
He bless my house
He bless my man.
But one thing hold my heart
It no lay down
Cause God ain't bless me one.
I no got pican by my side
To call me mommy."

Elisha say,
    "Nev mind, hyeah!
    I pray and God can bless you
    You going see."

The time pass.
The Shumanite be fat
And bye-m-bye she born a boy pican.
The pican do well
He run about the house.

He grow and walk behind him pa.
The small boy walk behind him pa
When the old man work in the rice

The sun be hot too much
The boy cry out
      "My head! My head!"
He fall down and he cry
And when they carry him for house
He no cry again.
Death put him hand on pican's heart
And hold him tight.

Elisha hear the word.
He send him stick to make the boy be well
But stick no got the plenty power
And pican die.

Elisha come
He pray
He send all people out.
Elisha put him mouth on pican mouth
He blow, he blow, he blow again.
He lay down hard on pican
And then he blow and blow some more.

The small boy go "kechew, kechew"
Seven times the pican go "kechew"
And then he laugh.
Death take him hand from off him heart.

Elisha see him move
And open up him eyes
He cry for mommy.

When the woman hear she pican cry
She run inside the house
And fall down low
And hold Elisha's foot
And thank him plenty.
But Elisha say
      "Nev mind
      It no be for me
      Cause this be God palaver.
      God give
      God take
      And God give again.
      Thank God!"

The Shushan King Love Peace

The Shushan king take Esther for him wife.
The king be proud to look on him new queen
And send the word to all them other kings.
And chiefs and head mens come to see
And when they look on Esther
All they hearts lay down
Cause she be beautiful past all
And she be fine.
The king he live in peace
But evil men be all about
To bring him trouble
And Haman be they leader.

Haman come in fore the king
He say
       "O King live forever!
       Now I must speak
       Cause what I say be true.
       In all the king's wide land
       In all the twenty nations
       And the hundred cities
       And the thousand towns
       In every place where good men hear the king
       And mind him word,

Another people live
And walk another way
And keep another law.
This no be good.

"In council we done talk palaver
And all the council say one thing
All the council agree
The people of that nation
What no mind your word
Must die."
The king love peace
But when him council speak
He hear the word.
The king take off him finger ring
And put the ring on Haman
And he say
        "The power be in you hand."

Then Haman make hard law
That on one day all men must rise
And kill the Hebrews.
All the Hebrews in the land
If they be old or young
Or man or woman kind
They all must die.
When Haman make the law
The council send it all about

And speakers speak the word
In street and market place
And Hebrews moan.

Now Esther be the queen
And all the people look on she
And never know she be a Hebrew gal
And that the Hebrew slave
What keep the king's front door
Be Uncle Mordecai to the queen.
Queen Esther every day look out
To see she uncle at the gate
And when she see him setting down to moan
She heart turn over.

When she savvy how the palaver lay
She grieve.
She pray.
She call she uncle and she say
     "For this
     God raise me up.
     For this
     God set me up in mansion house.
     For this
     I going go and stand up fore the king
     To beg him for my people.
     And if I die for this,
     I die."

Three days the queen no fix she face
She no take chop
She no talk nor sing a song
Three days.
And then she rise and wash
And make she woman rub she skin with oil
And comb she hair and make it sweet with scent.
She dress up fine with all new cloth
And stand up straight
And go in fore the king.

The Shushan king sit on him chair
And bout him stand the council
And the guard
And wise men.
When Queen Esther come
She look so fine
The king feel him heart grow big inside
But when he look the queen be sad
And so he call she close to speak.
She say
      "O King, live forever!
      You be good to me
      You be good too much
      And my love be plenty.
      So I come for say good-by
      And I going pray my God for bless you."

The king ain't savvy.
He say
>"How you talk so?
>Who say you can go?
>What side you think you go?
>And how you come for say good-by?"

Esther make she eyes big.
She say
>"Oh!
>You be the king
>You self do make the law.
>I no savvy why,
>I only say
>>'The king be my master.
>>When he say die
>>I die.' "

The king say
>"How you talk so?
>If you make play
>Then make it finish now
>Left small I vex."

But Esther say
>"My word no be for play.
>The law done fix
>The word done gone

On every road
That I must die
And all my Hebrew people with me.
And so I come
And so I say good-by."
Then the king see the thing
And he vex.
He mind how Haman talk the palaver
And now he make the law.

He rise up and he step down from him chair
And hold Queen Esther's hand
And say
      "Nev mind, hear,
      Now I see the thing.
      Nev mind, Esther Queen,
      I going fix it.
      You people no going die
      And you going live
      Close by you king
      And make him heart lay down."
That same day
New law go out from Shushan.
New law say
      "Any man what go to hurt a Hebrew
      The king will hang him!"

Now Haman done set up a post
In Shushan market place
And plot to hang
Queen Esther's Uncle Mordecai.
But when the day come
The king have soldiers take Haman
And hang him by him neck
On that same post
Till he be dead.

The Shushan king love peace
And with Queen Esther setting by him side
He rule the land
And evil men no come again.

Yam-Leaf Greens and Rice

Jacob work the farm
The sun make plenty hot
And other mens lay down and sleep
But Jacob work.

Esau hunt for meat
While Jacob work.
He run out in the bush all day
And he be tired.

Esau be the first-born son
In Isaac's house.
He play fool but Isaac love him plenty.
Jacob be the second-born
And he got sense.

Esau coming to the house
And passing by the farm
Where Jacob cutting bush.
Esau fall down on the ground and cry
        "O Jacob, my good brother!
        Help me now
        I beg you help me.
        Sick done catch me

Help me less I die."
Jacob drop him hoe
And run out from the field
To find him brother.

Esau call again
    "O Jacob, my good brother!
    I die just now if you no help.
    I die if you no give me chop—
    Bad hongry cramp done catch me."

Jacob look down on him brother and he vex.
Jacob say
    "How you do so?
    You lazy one!
    How you do we pa so bad?
    You be first-born son
    But you no carry first-born part.
    You run about like small boy
    You make play
    You no want work.
    How you do the old man so?"

Esau cry some more
    "O Jacob, my good brother!
    All them thing you say be true
    Cause you got plenty sense
    And I be fool.

But give me something for my belly now
Or turn you face away and lemme die."

Jacob go one side and come again
He say
    "See
    I got chop.
    I got yam-leaf greens and rice with plenty pepper.
    I got palm wine
    I got fruit
    But I going let you die.
    And when you dead
    All them first-born part going come to me."
Esau sniff and smell the greens.
Jacob shake the gourd
And Esau hear the palm wine guggle
And he think he die.
    "Give me chop for my belly!"
So he say
    "Give me chop!
    Take my first-born part
    If I live or if I die,
    But give me chop."
Jacob say
    "You swear?"

Esau say
> "I swear fore God,
> Now give me chop!"

Esau take the chop and wine
And make him belly tight
And then he sleep.

The years go by
And Old Man Isaac feel Death
Come inside him house.
He call out for him first-born son
To pass the word and bless him
And Jacob come and stand up side the bed
And Isaac say
> "Now I bless my first-born
> I give you all I got,
> God be my witness."
Jacob say
> "I thank you, Pa."
The old man say
> "I no can see
> But now I hear my Jacob's voice.
> Come by my side
> And let me feel you skin

Cause Esau's skin got plenty hair
    And Jacob's skin be clean."
The ma stand by
And quick she pass a goat-skin to she son
Who hold it on him arm and say
    "Pa, I come."

The old man reach him shaky hand
To feel the hair on Esau's skin
He feel the hair of goat and say
    "Thank God,
      I bless my first-born son
      And now I die in peace."
He turn him face to wall
And never move again.

So Esau play the fool
And trade the first-born part
To get him belly full
With yam-leaf greens and rice.

Old Satan Try Job Plenty

Lord God Almighty look on the world
And He see Satan walk about.
He say "Ah Satan! What side you come?"

Satan say
      "I come from Uz
      And there I see the man Job.
      He be big man for true-true.
      He got one thousand horses
      And two thousand cows
      And three thousand sheeps
      And four thousand goats
      And five thousand chickens."

God say
      "Job be one perfect man.
      I can give him plenty
      And I can love him,
      Cause he make my heart lay down.
      He be one perfect man."
Then Satan say
      "You call him perfect man,
      But take away the thing you give
      Let trouble live inside him house

Let all them thing go from him
You will see.
He will cuss you."

So it was that God make contract with Old Satan
To try Job's heart to see if he be good for true
Or if the things he got he love past God.
God take Him hand from off Job's house
And soldiers come and kill the people
And drive away the horses and the cattle.
And people come from other country
And take away the sheeps and all the goats.
Then other people come who see him weak
And take the chickens and the rice he got laid by.

And Job ain't savvy.

Then fire come, with wind, and burn
Him every house, all down,
And all him sons fall down and die
And all him gals,
And only left him wife.
Job heart turn over
He tear him robe
He paint him face to moan.
He say
        "Naked I born
        Naked I die

God give
God take.
Bless God!"

Satan come close and he humbug Job in him skin.
He make sores come on all him skin
And all the sores run pus
And plenty flies crawl on them
And every sore make smell.

Job's wife she come that time and say
    "Cuss God and die.
     Turn your back side to Him.
     Cuss God and die," she say.
Him big friends hear the word in every country.
Some say "What can I do?"
Some say "Big man, big trouble!"
Some say "It no be my palaver!"

But three friends come
And when they see, they tear they robes
And seven days and seven nights they set down
By they friend and mourn
And no man say one word.

Seven days they sit and no man don't say nothing.
Then one man raise him head and say

"I see the palaver how it be:
Evil live inside you heart
The thing you do and let man know is good
The thing you do what no be good
You think nobody knows.
But God can see them thing
And now you must confess
Or God will flog you more
And kill you too."

But Job say
      "No, it no be so.
      What I do for every man be good,
      And what I do for God be good.
      I no savvy why God do me so."
Satan humbug Job all that he can
And Job cry out and say
      "While my breath is in me
      My lips shall not speak wicked."

Lord God Almighty call Satan
And He say
      "Now you see what kind of man is Job.
      Now you see how come I care for him.
      Left him now so I can go and help him,
      Left him so I can lift him up."
Then God stoop down and tell Job nev mind.

He lift him up and wash him skin
And set him on him foot
And make him clean and strong again.

Job say "Bless God!"

He look about to make new house.
He walk about to find new cattle.
Each thing Job set him hand to do
Lord God Almighty put him hand there
And everything make double.

Job live long time again.
His woman bring new sons to call him pa.
He be rich man past all in Uz.
And all the people know
And all the people say
      "Lord God Almighty love Job,
      He be one perfect man!"

Brothers Got Bad Heart for Joseph

Joseph work in the rice farm.
Joseph and his brothers all work in the rice farm.
All cut new rice and tie new rice,
Joseph and his brothers.

And Joseph's bundle stand up straight.
He make proud
He walk about
He make like king.
The brothers' bundles fall down low
And make like slave.

The brothers see the thing and they vex,
They vex plenty.
They say
        "How come?
        How come the thing do so?
        Make it we mens must bow down for small boy?"

Joseph live in Canaan country.
He live in him pa house.
He no be small boy, again he no be man.

He be strong
He be clean
He be quick.
Joseph be fine young man.
He mind him pa's word
He make him pa's heart lay down.
Joseph have plenty brothers.
The brothers be old past Joseph.
They got they womens
They got they picans.
They no live in one house together
But all live close by.
All mind the old man's word
But they no love Joseph.
Joseph's pa be name Jacob.
Jacob be big man for Canaan country
He got plenty womens
He got plenty sons
He got plenty sheeps.

When the grass be finish in Canaan
Jacob tell him sons
    "Now you go and drive the sheeps.
    Bye-m-bye you find chop on other side
    Find new water
    Find new grass."

The sheeps be plenty

And the grass they find be small.
Every day they must go some more again.
They must go from the country where they belong.
They must go from they houses and they womens.
And they vex.

One moon pass.
Bye-m-bye they see young Joseph come.
They see him far off.
They know him cause he wear one fine coat,
It be one fine coat what Jacob make.
The old man done make the coat self.
It be fine with plenty colors
It be fine past all the coats them brothers got.

The brothers say
  "Ahah! Yon come that small boy.
  Yon come that humbug king.
  Yon he come."

Them brothers got bad heart for Joseph.

The brothers catch Joseph and they flog him.
They beat him good fashion.
He cry, he holler, and they beat him.
But one brother say
  "Wait!
  Now we kill him we no make pay.

Make it we find Mandingo trader
Mandingo man can take the boy,
Can carry Joseph to far country.
Mandingo man can pay we too."

And it was so.

Bye-m-bye the rain come again
And the grass grow green in every side
So the brothers turn back to they own country.

The brothers go together to they father's house
And they stand fore Jacob's face and say
   "Old man, our hearts cry for you this time.
   Our hearts cry for you cause we bring bad word.
   That side where we go find grass be bad for we
   That side be trouble country.

   "Strong mens walk about that side,
   Strong mens and big, they eat the mens what no be
   strong.
   And leopards live there, leopards big like elephants
   And snakes like trees go in the bush.
   In that country when one man walk
   Another man must walk, all two must walk together.
   So we live.

   "While we come we see one coat.

We pass, but the coat call.
We look him good
We see plenty colors.
Our hearts turn over.
Now we bring the coat so you can look him."

Jacob hold the coat
What he done make for Joseph
And he cry.

Now Joseph no be dead.
Them Mende mens carry him far.
They carry him cross the great dry sea.
They carry him for mighty Egypt
Where King Pharaoh make the law.
It be one big country,
Big past all other countries in that day.

Joseph be strong.
He be clean
He be quick
He be good boy.

First time he live for one big man house.
But woman palaver done catch him
And he go for jail.
In jail self he do good and God fight for Joseph.
God fight for him and bring him from the jail

And put him fore King Pharaoh's face.
King Pharaoh dream a dream:
Seven fat pigs come up from the river,
The pigs be fine and they live for a field
They eat grass and they hearts lay down.
Bye-m-bye seven poor, lean, dry, hongry pigs
Come from the river and go in the field.
The seven lean pigs eat the seven fat pigs
And when they finish they still be lean same way.

Joseph cry out "O King Pharaoh!"
So he cry out,
      "O King Pharaoh, it be true!
      My God do good for you.
      He make you see what come.
      Them seven fat pigs be seven fat years
      When Egypt going have plenty.
      Them seven lean pigs be seven lean years
      When Egypt going have nothing.
      That time the chop won't grow.
      That time the rain won't fall.
      That time hongry going catch the people
      And hongry going catch the cattle
      And plenty will die."
When King Pharaoh think good for him head
He make new law.

The word go in every town.
The word go in every palaver house.
>"This man Joseph," so the king say
>"This man Joseph be head man for all Egypt
>Save me one.
>What he say do, every man must do.
>And when he say come, every man must come.
>No man must lift up him hand or put down him foot
>But by Joseph word."

For true the land make plenty crop for seven years.
And Joseph make new tax so every town
And the country round every chief
Take up the rice and lay it by.
And every place the people build new warehouse.

When seven years of fat go by
Hongry time catch all the country.
Then all the people know that Joseph one
Can give them chop.
"This man Joseph!" all the people say.

From all the world the people come
And every kind of way the people talk
And every kind of gold they bring
And Joseph one must look them good
And say who get the rice and how much bags.

It come a day he walk for warehouse
He look about for everything
He stop.
He hear the Canaan talk
And Ho!
He see him brothers come to buy
Him heart turn over.
He no vex
The country talk be sweet.

He make proud
He make like king
The brothers fall down low
And make like slave.
He walk about and come again
He make a big palaver.
     "What side you come?"
He say in Egypt talk
     "Who be you pa?
     Who be you ma?
     I think so you be rogue.
     I think so I going kill you."

The speaker put the word in Canaan talk
The brothers fear and beg
And Joseph's heart grow big inside

He send all other people out
And he cry small.
The brothers look and wonder
But Joseph call each one by name
And then he say in Canaan talk
    "This man Joseph be you brother."

The brothers no can speak
They no can see the place they be
They see rice farm in Canaan land
And Joseph's bundle like a king
They see Mandingo traders with a slave
And Old Man Jacob with a coat
But Joseph softly, softly say
    "Nev mind.
      God's hand done fix the thing."

Wise Sword Find True Mommy

That time when Solomon be king
For all the Judah people
The country self be rich.
And in that time
They build new temple
Where priests make prayers and sacrifice.
They build new house for government
For council rooms and court
And all palaver.

King Solomon be wise too much
And when he speak him word the people mind
And every place he put him hand
The thing do well.
And kings from other place come there
And wise men come
And prophets come
To sit down in him court
And hear him word.

Two women go in fore the king
To bring palaver.
One be fat and one be lean
All two be so-so vex.

King Solomon say
    "Speak!"

First time the lean one say
    "O King Solomon!
    When you look on me
    You see you slave
    What mind you word.
    I no make palaver
    But that one there
    She bring the thing
    Up fore you face.
    Now you going see.

    "This fat and ugly gal
    She go for thief my pican.
    She want take him from my hand.
    I say no.
    She hold me and she holler
    I say no.
    She want beat me
    She want kill me
    For my pican
    I say no.

    "Make it, O King,
    You tell this woman left me.
    Make it, O King,

I beg you tell this woman
Take she hands from off my son."

The king say
        "I hear you."
He turn to other side and say
        "Speak you word."

The woman say
        "First time I hold my pican in my hand
        He be so fine
        He cry strong
        He catch teaty strong
        He be fine too much and fat same way.

        "Same time that lean mommy hold she pican
        And he be lean
        He be dry
        He be weak.
        Then fever come
        And catch that small one
        The fever shake him
        And he die.
        In the night
        The woman put she pican dead by me
        And she take my one,
        My fat strong pican
        Him she take.
        Now I say

'Give me back what belong me'
She say no.
So the palaver be."

King Solomon be wise.
He know them other kings
What sit down there
The wise mens and the prophets
Wait to hear what he say.

He look about.
All two the womens cry they word be true.
The king say
      "Bring the pican."

All two the womens say one time
      "You see he belong me one!"

The king say
      "Bring sharp sword."
King Solomon be wise.
He rise up from him chair
One hand lift the pican high
One hand lift the sword.
He say
      "Now I cut the palaver
      Now I cut the pican same way.
      One side go for lean mommy
      One side go for fat mommy
      So it be!"

Lean mommy say
      "So it be!"

Fat mommy fall down
She cry
      "No, I beg you no do so!"
Fat mommy laying there
She holding King Solomon foot
She crying
      "Give the pican to lean mommy
      But let him live
      Let the small one live
      I beg you!"
King Solomon be wise.
He look on the lean woman
And he say
      "Go from my face
      You wa-wa thing!
      Go from me fore I flog you!"

All them other kings
What sit down there
The wise mens and the prophets
Know King Solomon be wise.

All people know
True mommy no can say
      "Kill my son!"

The Babylonia Princes Vex

First time
Daniel be a slave in Babylon.
But Daniel savvy God
And mind God's Word
And so God bless him.

God give Daniel plenty sense
All the people round him see
And when new king go for mansion house
The king call Daniel.

The king raise Daniel up
And put him over every prince
And over every chief
And Daniel do well.

But the Babylonia princes vex.
They vex to see a slave be high
And so they make a plot.
They dassn't say he no can do.
They dassn't say he no got sense.
He no tell lie

He never play the rogue.
They look him good.

They look him and they see
He bow down to him God and pray
He ever bow him down.
The princes say "Ahah!"
They walk in fore the king and say they need new law
To make all people bow down to the king
And him one only.
The king agree.

Then they say the king must make the law with force
And any man who no do so
They throw him to the lions for chop.
The king agree.

Then they say the king must make a paper
And must send the law to every place in Babylon
So all can know.
And the king agree.

Bye-m-bye the princes bring Daniel with soldiers.
They bring him fore the king.
They say
      "This slave man you done set up over we,
      He no keep you law.

He no bow down to you one and only.
Make it we pass him to the lions."

The king feel him heart turn over
He look all about
He hold him head.
He love Daniel but him hand be tied
The law done put for paper.
And so he say
    "I agree."

The king see soldiers carry Daniel from the court
Out to the place they keep the lions.
The king go in him house and cry.
All day the king no take him chop
All night the king say "Make no music."

Soon in the morning time
Soon fore sun wake up
The king move out from mansion house
Out to the place where lions live.

He come close by
He don't hear nothing.
He make the guard take off the rock
What cover up the hole.
He call for Daniel

Then he hear
  "O King live forever!
  My God send angels here
  To care for me."

The king look
And it be so.
The king cry out
  "For true,
  Daniel's God be master over kings
  And God of Gods."
And Daniel say
  "For true."

Joshua Be God's Man

When Moses die
Then Joshua take the lead
For all the Hebrew people
And Joshua hear God's word and mind
And God be with him.

Plenty times the Hebrews fight
And Joshua lead in war
To take the Canaan land
And make the Hebrews strong.

The Hebrews wander all about in bush and field
And come to Jericho
What be a city built inside a wall
Like one big house
And strong.

When they see the Hebrews come
Them Canaan people run inside the wall
And close the door.

Joshua come up close and knock.
The door man say
        "Who that?"

Joshua say
>"It be me, Joshua
>I be good man
>I be head man for Hebrew people.
>Open up you door so we can come inside
>And sit down by you fire
>And sleep inside you house.
>Open up.
>I be God's man
>My people be God's people
>Open up and God going bless you."

Now them Canaan people
Never know true God
When Joshua say
>"God going bless you"
Them Canaan people laugh.
They say
>"Go from we door
>You dirty bush man.
>Go from we door
>We no want mess with you
>You no can come inside.
>Go from we door
>You dirty bush man."

Joshua vex to hear the people say
That he be bush man.

Joshua call on God
And God give him the word.
Just how God say
So Joshua make the people do
He lead them and they follow.

They walk all about the Jericho wall
One time they walk around
And priests walk with the fighting men
And priests blow horns.

The next day it be just the same
They walk around again
And priests walk with the fighting men
And blow they horns.
The next day just the same
And then the next
Till six days finish so
Then Joshua give the word
That on the next day
When they walk one time around
Then all the men must shout out loud
And all the priests must blow they horns
And all the women, all the boys and gals
Must sing and shout.
Seven times they walk about the wall
Seven times then they sing and shout.

Seven times they walk about the wall.
And when they go to sing and shout
The wall go on one side
And then the other side.
He break in one place
Then he break in nother place
He fall down here
He fall down over there.
And then he fall down altogether,
Broke in small small pieces like some sand.
And wind rise up and blow
And no man see
And all the Hebrew people cry out
"God Almighty fight for we!"
The wind blow by
And where the city put a wall
The people see a road.
So while the fighting men go in
And kill the Canaan people there
The priests walk all about
Walking on the road.
They walk all about and they sing
They walk all about the Jericho road
They walk all about and they sing and shout.

Every Man Heart Lay Down

Long time past
Before you papa live
Before him papa live
Before him pa's papa live—

Long time past
Before them big tree live
Before them big tree's papa live—
That time God live.

And God look on the world
What He done make
And Him heart no lay down.
And He walk about in the town
To see the people
And He sit down in the palaver house
To know the people
And He vex too much.
And God say
    "Nev mind.
    The people no hear My Word
    The people no walk My way
    Nev mind.
    I going break the world and lose the people

I going make the day dark
And the night I going make hot.
I going make water that side where land belong
And land that side where water belong.
And I going make a new country
And make a new people."
Now this time
God's one small boy—Him small pican—hear God's Word
And the pican grieve for people
So he go fore God's face
And make talk for him Pa.
     "Pa, I come for beg You," so he say
     "I come for beg You,
     Don't break the world
     What You done make.
     Don't lose the people
     What You done care for.
     I beg You
     Make it I go
     I talk to people
     I walk with people
     Bye-m-bye they savvy the way."

And the pican go down softly softly
And hold God's foot.
So God look on Him small boy
And Him heart be soft again
And God say

"Aye My son,
When you beg me so
I no can vex.
Left me now, but hear me good:
If you go you must be born like a man
And you must live like a man
And you must have hurt and have hunger.
And hear me good:
Men will hate you
And they will flog you
And bye-m-bye they will kill you
And I no going put My hand there."

And the pican say
    "I agree!"

And bye-m-bye God call Mary
To be Ma for the pican.
Now Mary be new wife for Joseph
And Joseph ain't touch Mary self
So first time Joseph vex.
But God say
    "Nev mind, Joseph,
    This be God palaver."
    And Joseph heart lay down.

And God see one king who try for do good
For all him people

And God say
        "Ahah, Now I send My son
        For be new king."
        And God send star to call the king.

And in a far country
God hear a wise man call Him name
And God say to the wise man
        "I send My son to be new wise man,
        Go now with the star."
And the star call
And the wise man follow.

And by the waterside
Men lay down for take rest
And they hear fine music in the sky
Like all the stars make song,
And they fear.
And all the dark make bright like day
And the water shine like fire
And no man can savvy
And they hearts turn over.
But God's angel come
And God's angel say
        "Make glad, all people,
        God's pican be born in Bethlehem."
And the people say "Oh."

And the wise man and the king
And the country people come to Bethlehem
And the star come low and stop.
But when they go for mansion house
The star no be there.
And when they go for Big Man's house
The star no be there.
And bye-m-bye when they go for hotel
The star no be there gain—
But the wise man say
      "Ahah, the star be by the small house
      Where cattle sleep!"
And it was so.

And they find Joseph and Mary
And the small small pican
Fold up in country cloth
And the king bring gold for gift
And the wise man bring fine oil
And the country people bring new rice.

And they look on the God pican
And every man heart lay down.

Small Boy Teach Wise Men

When Jesus still be small boy
All the people see He got plenty sense
And they no savvy how it be
But Jesus savvy.

Jesus be small but He know Lord God Almighty.
He savvy all the God palaver
Cause Him self be God's Own Son.
But the people they no savvy.

First time Jesus live on Africa side
Him Pa, Him Ma and the small pican.
Joseph bring all them cross the waters.
They cross the dry seas
And they set down in Africa
While Jesus grow.

The boy grow fine and clean
And every place Joseph go the boy go 'long
And Joseph walk proud.
Bye-m-bye the time come
For go back to Judah land
Him Pa, Him Ma, and small boy go.
And Jesus be fine and wise same way.

Now all the Judah people like Jerusalem.
The king live in fine mansion house
And holy priests make sacrifice
Inside the temple wall.

The king send out him word.
He say
      "Come to Jerusalem!"
And the Judah people rise and go.
The place be full too much
Cause people come from every side.

They come to Jerusalem
They come on horse
They come on camel
They come on foot
Plenty people come.

Some people bring fine things to trade
And make big market in the street.
Some make show
And some make music.
Plenty sing and dance.

That time Joseph take him wife and small boy.
He take all him people and go.
He go for government house and call him name
And pay him tax.

He go for temple and take him sacrifice to burn.
The priest bless him and bless him house.

Joseph go for market and he trade.
He find plenty friend and he say how do
And he take small chop and drink small wine.
Sometime he move about and see Mary
Sometime he see Jesus
Sometime he lose all two.

Bye-m-bye the palaver be finish in Jerusalem
And Joseph call him people.
He say
      "Make it we go now!
      All them people from my town
      Make it we go now!"
And him people move out
But the boy Jesus no be there.

The people walk. They walk. They walk.
Joseph walk with the mens
And Mary walk with the womens.
All day they walk.
When the sun go for sleep
Joseph find Mary and he say
      "Mary, where the small boy?"

But Mary ain't see him.
The boy done lost
And Mary vex.

They no go back that same night
Cause robbers wait by the road.
But morning time come and they go quick.

And when they come for city
They go for market place
But Jesus no be there.
They go nother side
Where small boys set down
And old men tell they stories
But they no see Jesus.

Then they go for temple
What be God's own house
And the boy Jesus be there.

They find Him setting down
And all about Him wise men stand
And priests
And them what know the book,
And Jesus telling them 'bout God palaver.

Plenty people look and wonder
And they say,
      "Oh!
      The small boy know something!
      The small boy savvy!
      He know all the book
      And he know all the law."

Then Mary move in past the big mens
And she say
      "How you do we so?
      All night and all day we fear for you.
      How you do we so?"

And Jesus say
      "You ain't savvy this be God palaver?
      You ain't savvy
      For this I come
      For this I live
      For this I die?
      You ain't savvy?"

God Make Plenty Chop

Jesus walk about
And where He go
Plenty people come behind.

They bring the ones who no can see
And Jesus make they eyes open.
They bring the ones who no can walk
And Jesus make them straight and strong.
Sometime they bring dead ones
And Jesus make them live again.

Plenty people follow Him.
He give them God's own word
And it be sweet.

One day He sit down on a mountain side
And five thousand people be there to hear.
He say
       "Lord God Almighty got plenty fine house
       What hands ain't make,
       And plenty thing for fit your mouth
       What farm ain't grow,

And fine sweet water
Like spring ain't never give,
And plenty palm wine too."

The talk be sweet
The people stay to hear the word
Til hongry catch them.
One Jesus friend say
    "Make it they go away and find chop.
    We no can feed they."
Jesus say
    "Nev mind
    God got plenty chop to fit they mouth."
Then Jesus say
    "Every man must bring a gift for God."
One small boy say
    "For true."
Jesus say
    "Now you bring your gift?"
Small boy say
    "I can give Him what small I got,
    Five cakes
    And two small fishes."

While all the people look
Jesus bless the cakes and them two fishes.

Five thousand people sit down there.
They see Him break the chop
The people see small chop grow
And He send out baskets
Every basket full.

Five cakes and two small fishes grow
Cause God done bless the chop.
Jesus know God palaver,
And God make plenty
So nobody don't be hongry.